STORYTIME COLLECTION

This book belongs to

_____

_____

Autumn
Publishing

Published in 2019
by Autumn Publishing
Cottage Farm
Sywell
NN6 0BJ
www.igloobooks.com

GUA009 0419
2 4 6 8 10 9 7 5 3 1
ISBN 978-1-78905-239-8

Printed and manufactured in China

Disney · PIXAR
FINDING
DORY

〰 STORYTIME COLLECTION 〰

When she was young, Dory, a blue tang fish, lived happily with her parents in a cosy coral home. But there was one problem – Dory struggled to remember things.

Her parents, wanting to keep Dory safe, would help her
practise introducing herself. "Hi, I'm Dory. I suffer
from short-term memory loss," she would say
again and again.

One day, despite her parents' warnings, Dory wandered off and forgot where she was and what she was doing. She tried asking other fish for help, but couldn't remember anything about herself. Years passed, by which time, Dory had completely forgotten about her parents.

As Dory travelled around the Great Barrier Reef, she bumped into a clownfish called Marlin, who was looking for his son, Nemo. Together, the pair went on an amazing journey to rescue Nemo, and had lots of exciting adventures.

Once they'd found Marlin's son, all three came back to live at the Great Barrier Reef. Dory lived in a coral cave next door to Marlin and Nemo's anemone home. The three were best friends and always made sure they looked out for one another.

Dory would often go with Nemo to school, and loved joining the teacher, Mr. Ray, and the younger fish, on trips around the Reef. Today, they were watching stingray migrating. "Migration is about going home," said Mr. Ray.

After listening to Mr. Ray speak, Dory said to herself, "My parents, where are they?" As she thought about her family, Dory drifted closer and closer to the stingrays...

... before she knew it, Dory was sucked into the undertow. As she was bumped around, images of her parents flashed into Dory's mind. Then, she passed out.

Dory woke up suddenly. "I remember my family!" she cried. Dory told Marlin and Nemo that her parents lived in Morro Bay, California.

Dory was upset when she realised how far away it was, but Marlin knew someone who could help.

"Woo-hoo!" shouted Crush. He was the sea turtle who had helped Marlin and Dory travel to Sydney to find Nemo. Now he was helping take the three fish along the ocean current to California.

Dory and Nemo were enjoying the journey, but Marlin wasn't finding it much fun. "I'm going to be sick," he groaned. To his relief, they soon reached Morro Bay. Saying goodbye to Crush, the three fish jumped off his shell and tumbled out of the current.

With her friends' help, Dory began exploring the area. "Mum! Dad!" she cried, as they travelled through a sunken ship. A hermit crab shushed Dory, causing another memory to flash through her mind.

"Jenny!" she suddenly shouted. "Charlie!" Dory remembered her parents' names. However, her shouts had also woken a giant squid!

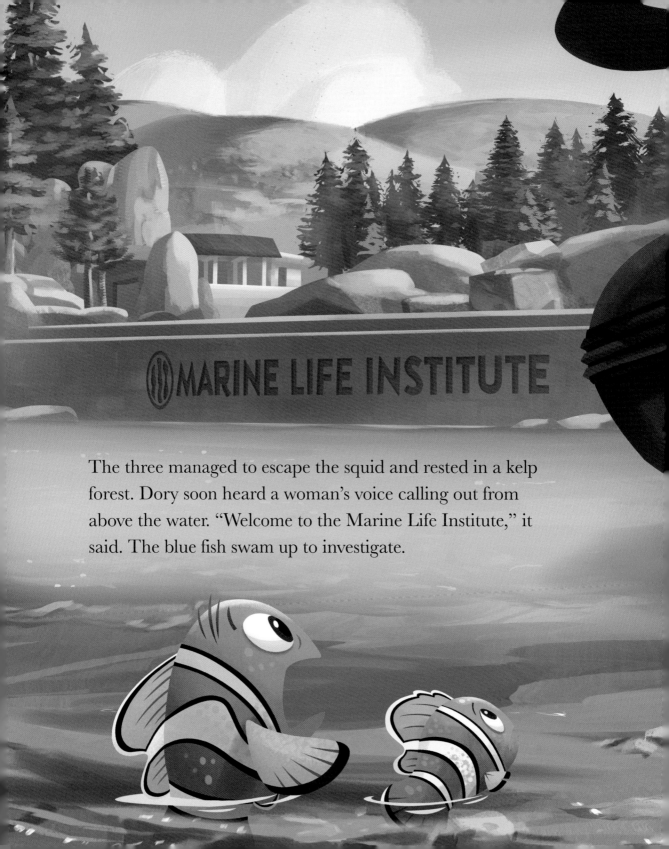

MARINE LIFE INSTITUTE

The three managed to escape the squid and rested in a kelp forest. Dory soon heard a woman's voice calling out from above the water. "Welcome to the Marine Life Institute," it said. The blue fish swam up to investigate.

Just as Marlin and Nemo headed up to join her, Dory was snatched out of the water and taken away!

Dory was taken inside a building where she had an orange tag put on her fin and was then placed inside a tank. Dory soon met an octopus called Hank. He explained that the tag meant she'd be taken to Cleveland. Dory panicked. "I have to get to the Jewel of Morro Bay, California and find my family!" she cried.

"That's this place," said Hank, who offered Dory a deal. He wanted to go to Cleveland, so needed Dory's tag. In return, he'd help Dory find her parents.

Outside the Institute, Marlin and Nemo were asking two helpful sea lions, Fluke and Rudder, about the building. "It's a fish hospital," said Fluke, happily.

"How are we going to get inside?" asked Nemo.

"You want to get inside?" asked Rudder.

"Desperately," replied Marlin.

The two sea lions knew exactly how to help.
"Oo-roo. Ooo-roo-roo," they yelled into the sky.

Meanwhile, Hank took Dory to a map of the Institute so she could find where her parents lived. As she looked at the map, she saw a purple shell and another memory came to her.

Dory used to line shells up with her parents. Purple ones were her mother's favourite. Moments later, a human carrying a bucket of fish came down the hall. The bucket had 'DESTINY' written on it. Dory felt this was a sign. "We've got to get in that bucket," she said. Before Hank could stop her, Dory leapt inside and was taken away.

DESTINY

After a short journey, Dory was thrown into a
pool where a whale shark called Destiny lived.
When Dory spoke to her in whale, Destiny
instantly recognised her.

"We'd talk through the pipes when we were little," said Destiny. More importantly, she knew the exact exhibit where Dory had lived.

Dory was then introduced to Bailey, a beluga whale who claimed his echolocation didn't work. "What's echolocation?" asked Dory.

"Bailey's head puts out a call, and the echo helps him find objects far away," replied Destiny.

Just then, Hank splashed in the pool and asked for Dory's tag. However, the blue tang still needed to find her parents. "Follow me," said Dory, who knew how Hank could help.

Back on the rock outside, Fluke and Rudder introduced Marlin and Nemo to a crazy-looking bird. "Lads, meet Becky," said Fluke, who explained the only way inside the Institute was to fly. "Look her in the eye and say 'ooo-roo' and she'll be in sync with you," added the sea lion.

Marlin went, "Ooo-roo," and soon he and Becky were the best of friends.

Becky then picked up Marlin and Nemo using a green bucket.
"This is nuts!" cried Marlin, as Becky
lifted them up into the sky.

At the Institute, Hank and Dory had made their way from Destiny's tank to a touch-pool. Lots of little hands plunged into the water and started poking Hank, who released some ink, turning the water black.

Escaping through the inky water, Dory and Hank made their way to the surface. The Open Ocean exhibit was straight ahead. Putting Dory in a plastic cup left by one of the children, Hank swung across the ceiling and dropped Dory into the tank where her parents lived.

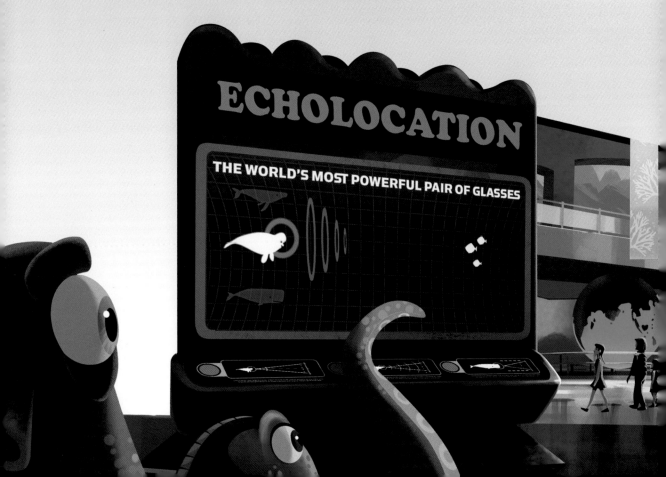

ECHOLOCATION

THE WORLD'S MOST POWERFUL PAIR OF GLASSES

Meanwhile, Becky carried the bucket, with Marlin and Nemo inside, towards the Institute. However, when she saw some popcorn on the floor, Becky left the bucket on a tree, leaving Marlin and Nemo stranded as she swooped down to eat the tasty snack.

Knowing Dory always had a plan for situations like this, they both asked, "What would Dory do?" The pair of clownfish looked around for anything that could help. Soon, they noticed a row of fountains stretching across the plaza. Without waiting a moment longer, the pair jumped out of the bucket and hopped along the streams of water until they reached some drain pipes that led inside the Institute.

In the Open Ocean exhibit,
Dory came across a path of shells.
She followed it and arrived at her childhood home!
Once there, all her early memories came flooding back,
including how she was forced apart from her parents. When Dory was
younger, she had been swimming towards a purple shell, got sucked into
the undertow and pulled into the pipes. From there, she'd ended up alone
in the open ocean.

Dory was snapped out of her memories by a voice. "Where's your tag?" it asked. Dory turned and saw two crabs. They explained to her that all the blue tangs were in Quarantine and were going to be taken to Cleveland. The only way to get there was through the pipes. "It's two lefts and a right," said one of the crabs.

Knowing it was the only way to reach her parents, Dory took
a deep breath and went into the pipes. However, despite repeating
the instructions to herself again and again, she was soon lost.
Quickly remembering her pipe pal, Destiny, Dory called out
for help. "Destineeeeee!" Dory cried out in whale.

In order to help Dory, Destiny convinced Bailey to try using his echolocation. The beluga whale quickly realised it wasn't broken after all, and was soon guiding Dory safely through the pipes. Then, a shadow approached Dory from out of the murky waters. Bailey was afraid his friend was about to be attacked when the blue tang cried out, "It's okay! I found Marlin and Nemo!"

Marlin and Nemo helped Dory reach Quarantine. Seeing the blue tangs at the far end of a row of fish tanks, the three friends hopped across until they'd reached their destination.

Once inside the tank, Dory looked around for her parents. They weren't there. The other blue tangs told Dory her parents had come to Quarantine to look for their daughter years ago and hadn't been seen since. Dory couldn't believe it. "I'm all alone," she said, sadly.

Hank appeared and pulled Dory out of the tank just before it was loaded on to the truck. However, Nemo and Marlin were still inside. Before the octopus could grab them, he was picked up by a human, forcing him to drop Dory, who fell down a drain that led into the ocean.

Just like when she was younger, Dory found
herself alone in the ocean. As she swam around
aimlessly, Dory came across a row of shells dotted along
the ocean floor. "I like shells," she said, and so decided to
follow them. As Dory got closer, she saw the shells led to a
home inside a tyre. It was then she noticed more paths made from
shells leading out in every direction. The curious blue tang looked
around, but saw no one. Then, two figures appeared in the distance…

... it was Dory's parents! The pair rushed over to
hug their daughter. "You found us,"
said her mother, happily.

"I'm never letting you go again," said her father, as he held her tight. Dory's parents then told her how they made these shell paths, knowing she would find them one day.

"And do you know why you found us?" said Jenny. "Because you remembered in your own amazing Dory way."

Dory then quickly remembered that her other family, Marlin and Nemo, were on their way to Cleveland.

On the truck, Marlin and Nemo thought they'd seen Dory in one of the tanks, but it was only Hank camouflaging himself. "I'm sorry," said Hank. "I tried to hold on, but I lost her." Marlin and Nemo were sad at the thought of not only being taken to Cleveland, but that they'd never see Dory again.

Meanwhile, Dory and her parents had surfaced outside the Institute. The truck had gone, but Dory had a plan to find it. "Destineeeeee!" cried out Dory.

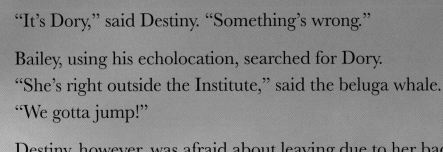

"It's Dory," said Destiny. "Something's wrong."

Bailey, using his echolocation, searched for Dory.
"She's right outside the Institute," said the beluga whale.
"We gotta jump!"

Destiny, however, was afraid about leaving due to her bad
eyesight. "I'll never make it out there!" she cried.

"I will be your eyes," said Bailey, who then whispered,
"It's your destiny, Destiny."

So, without wasting another second, Destiny
and Bailey leapt over the wall and into
the ocean to find Dory.

Dory, Jenny, Charlie, Destiny and Bailey
raced after the truck, hoping to reach the
bridge before the vehicle did. Once they
reached the bridge, they needed a plan so
they could get on board. "If only there was
a way to stop traffic!" cried Bailey.

"Stop traffic," muttered Dory, as she looked
at a group of otters. Suddenly, an idea came
to her. "I got it!" she cried, and swam over to
the happy mammals.

Held safely in the paws of one of the
otters, Dory was taken up onto the bridge and onto the road.
Once there, she and the otters had a cuddle party. "So cute!" cried
all the drivers, as they stopped their vehicles to watch the animals hug.

With the truck now stuck in traffic, the otter holding Dory took her to the
back of the vehicle.

The otter passed Dory to Hank, who put her in Marlin and Nemo's tank. "I never thought we'd see you again," said Nemo.

"I couldn't leave my family," said Dory, as the three fish hugged.

Just then, the driver appeared, shooing the otters away.
"Oh, no," said Dory. "There goes our ride."

"Leave it to me," said Marlin. "I got this. Oo-roo! Oo-roo!" he called.

Moments later, Becky appeared, holding the green bucket. But she
only took Marlin and Nemo. Dory and Hank were left behind.

Dory was stranded on the truck
with Hank. "It's over," said the octopus, sadly.

"No, there's got to be a way," said Dory, who noticed
a vent in the roof of the truck. She and Hank squeezed
through and the octopus stretched himself across the
windshield. The driver slammed on the brakes and jumped
out of the truck. Hank took the driver's seat, while Dory
gave directions. "Follow those seagulls!" she cried, knowing
they'd lead them straight to the ocean.

Before long, Dory could see the ocean below. With no other way of getting everyone to the open sea, Hank drove the truck off the edge of the road. As it flipped in the air, the doors opened and all the fish fell out of their tanks and splashed safely into the sea. Hank grabbed Dory in mid-air, and they both smiled as they fell towards the water.

With her latest adventure over, Dory, her parents, Marlin, Nemo, Hank,
Destiny and Bailey, returned to the Great Barrier Reef. Dory was so
happy to have all her friends and family together for the first time.

One morning, a little while after returning home, Dory swam to the edge of the reef with Marlin. "It really is quite a view," said her friend.

"Unforgettable," replied Dory, who couldn't remember the last time she felt so happy.

THE END

COLLECT THEM ALL!

With 12 more exciting titles to choose from, you'll want to complete your Storytime Collection!

Can Aladdin and Jasmine stop the evil Jafar?

Will Bambi learn the value of friendship?

Will Belle be able to break the curse?

How far will a father go for his son?

Can Anna and Elsa stop an eternal winter?

Will Mowgli defeat Shere Khan?

Will the Incredibles save the day?

Will Simba ever become king?

Will Ariel be able to find her prince in time?

Can Moana restore the heart of Te Fiti?

Will Maleficent's curse come true?

Will Rapunzel learn who she truly is?